Grumpy King Colin

Maverick
Early Readers

'Grumpy King Colin'
An original concept by Phil Allcock
© Phil Allcock

Illustrated by Steve Stone

Published by MAVERICK ARTS PUBLISHING LTD

Studio 3A, City Business Centre, 6 Brighton Road,

Horsham, West Sussex, RH13 5BB

© Maverick Arts Publishing Limited February 2016

+44 (0)1403 256941

A CIP catalogue record for this book is available at the British Library.

ISBN 978-1-84886-194-7

arts publishing
www.maverickbooks.co.uk

This book is rated as: Turquoise Band (Guided Reading)
The original picture book text for this story has been modified
by the author to be an early reader.

Grumpy
King Colin

by Phil Allcock

illustrated by Steve Stone

King Colin felt grumpy. For breakfast he
had lettuce on toast, with cold gravy.

"You can't eat that!" said Queen Christine.

"I can," said King Colin. And he did, because he could, because he was king.

Silly King Colin.

Later, he went to the toilet without washing his hands. "You can't do that!" Queen Christine said.

"I can," said King Colin. And he did,

because he could, because he was king.

Dirty King Colin.

He picked up an old shirt that smelled of
fish stew and cabbage.

"You can't wear that – it stinks!" said Queen Christine.

"I can," said King Colin. And he did, because he could, because he was king.

Smelly King Colin.

King Colin was bored ...

so he decided to go for a ride.

His favourite horse, Pink Nose the Third,

was in the stables.

But Pink Nose the Third had no saddle.

King Colin had a tantrum.

He jumped up and down, shouting,

"Where's my horse's saddle?"

"Daddy, no one knew you were going for a ride!" said Prince Pete. "You can't shout like that!"

"I can," said King Colin.

And he did, because he could,

because he was king.

Grumpy King Colin.

King Colin rode into the country.

He trotted straight through

a field of cabbages.

"You can't do that!" shouted the farmer.

"I can," said King Colin. And he did,

because he could, because he was king.

Rude King Colin.

Soon, King Colin reached a big pool of mud. "Can I make Pink Nose the Third jump over that?" he thought.

"Yes, I can," he decided. And he did,

because he could, because he was king.

Crazy King Colin.

Suddenly Pink Nose dug his hooves in and
stopped. King Colin fell off.

His face went as red as a tomato.

He roared louder than
the loudest lion ...
but no one heard him.

King Colin stomped home.

"Daddy, you can't go upstairs in your dirty boots," said Princess Penny.

"I can," snapped King Colin. And he did,

because he could, because he was king.

Naughty King Colin.

King Colin had sausages and beans with custard for lunch.

"You can't eat that!" said Queen Christine.

King Colin was still cross. "I can!" he roared.

"Oh no, you can't!" said a voice.

It was Great Queen Connie.

"Colin, you've been...

silly, dirty, smelly, grumpy, rude, crazy

and naughty. I'm sending you straight

to your room!"

"You can't do that!" said King Colin.

"I can," said Great Queen Connie.

And she did, because she could,

because she was the King's mum.

The End

Quiz

1. What does King Colin have with his lettuce and toast?
a) Cold gravy
b) Baked beans
c) Strawberry jam

2. What is the name of King Colin's horse?
a) Red Hoof the Fourth
b) Blue Eyes the Second
c) Pink Nose the Third

3. What type of field does King Colin ride through?
a) A cabbage field
b) A carrot field
c) A corn field

4. What does King Colin do that is naughty?
a) Slam the door
b) Walk upstairs with dirty boots
c) Slide down the stairs

5. What is King Colin's punishment for being grumpy?
a) He has to clean the stables
b) He has to apologise to everyone
c) He gets sent to his room

Turn over for answers

Maverick Early Readers

Our early readers have been adapted from the original picture books so that children can make the essential transition from listener to reader. All of these books have been book banded, for guided reading, to the industry standard and edited by a leading educational consultant.

Green Band

Yuck! Said the Yak Early Reader
ISBN 978-1-84886-176-3

I Wish I'd Been Born a Unicorn Early Reader
ISBN 978-1-84886-196-1

Orange Band

The Black and White Club Early Reader
ISBN 978-1-84886-179-4

Gold Star for George Early Reader
ISBN 978-1-84886-197-8

A Scarf and a Half Early Reader
ISBN 978-1-84886-177-0

Pirates Don't Drive Diggers Early Reader
ISBN 978-1-84886-195-4

Turquoise Band

Preposterous Rhinoceros Early Reader
ISBN 978-1-84886-180-0

Hocus Pocus Diplodocus Early Reader
ISBN 978-1-84886-178-7

Grumpy King Colin Early Reader
ISBN 978-1-84886-194-7

The Four Little Pigs Early Reader
ISBN 978-1-84886-193-0

Quiz Answers: 1a, 2c, 3a, 4b, 5c